Hi! This story was written by me; George Port.

I am 10 years old and I love imagination and adventure! I aspire to be a famous author one day.

I hope you enjoy the story

Chapter One:
What is going on at school?!

Miss Quin was being slightly odd that day; she looked stressed and shouted at Logan to stop picking his nose. "Make it neater!" she said peering at our science workbooks. Miss Quinn is never usually this fussy, but that day must be an exception for her, which is strange as I thought Miss Quinn was usually really cheery on Thursdays. I guess that just wasn't a good Thursday.

"Do you think somethings up with Miss Quinn" I asked Mia, who sits to the right of me.

"Hmm, oh, I am not completely sure, she is being a bit weird" she replied.

"A bit Weird!" said Tilly, who sits to the left of me.

"Weird? I know the definition of weird, and that, is far from weird, not even close".

She pointed at Miss Quinn and said "she is obviously mildly stressed about something". She said this a little too loudly and Miss Quinn turned to look at us.

"It's alright" I said, "it's not like she can hear us, she is all the way over there".

"Well, I must have very good hearing then, mustn't I George Port!" Ops!

"Go and move your name down George" Miss Quinn shouted at me.

At Hampton we have this thing called a learning ladder. At the start of the year, you write your name on a peg and it gets moved up and down a ladder depending upon your behaviour; outstanding, great effort, ready to learn, wrong choice and time out. I slowly trudged over to the door of the class room, taking my time. I really didn't care, or at least I told myself I didn't care. "Now!!!!!! She yelled again, even louder than before.

Now I don't want you to get the wrong impression of Miss Quinn. She is usually a really nice person. I mean, I've seen her angry before, but never this angry. On the whole, the last time she was properly angry was last week when a kid in my class, Asher, snuck over to Flynn and dared him to stick his whole hand in his month, which he did.

I was outside the door and moving my name down.

"Hurry up George!" Miss Quinn shouted.

"I'm coming" I said and pondered why Miss Quinn was in such a bad mood. Miss Quinn continued to be in a bad mood all day and so did all the other teachers. They were all stomping around and frowning and yelling, even at the littlest thing. Ben G in Miss Thurgood's class accidentally dropped a pea whilst eating lunch, and Miss Miles made him miss his whole lunch break!

Me, Cian, Harry and Jaiden (my best mates) were talking about how all the teachers were in a bad mood that day.

"It's probably just nothing" said Jaiden to us.

"Just nothing?!" I said "Just nothing, have you not noticed that all the teachers are in a bad mood all on the same day?! I'm pretty sure somethings up".

Harry said, "It might just be a school inspector or something like that, maybe".

"Meh, dunno", replied Cian, they are in a pretty bad mood and I have not seen any inspectors. Perhaps it's a full moon today and they are all secretly werewolves".

We all laughed and did some quiet howling. Quiet so that none of the moody teachers hear us and shout at us.

"Maybe, they have heard from the government that they have to change the damned curriculum again" Harry suggested and we all nodded in agreement. It was all a bit strange, but I guessed that we would find out sometime, and I guessed right.

Chapter Two:
Do I just have an overactive imagination?

I walked from breakfast club into the class room the next day, feeling a sense that we might get a day off classes, because all around the classroom they had taken all the tables apart. Now, to make the whole table the teachers put three smaller tables together, making it look like one big one. When year 6 kids do tests, they do it in our classrooms with the tables split apart for exam conditions. This was strange as I didn't think Year 6 had any exams coming up. When this happens, we, the year 5s, get shifted off to the library to work, which I actually quite like.

I had been so busy trying to work out why the tables were separated; I had not realised that I was in the classroom alone. Since I never get to do this, I picked up Miss Quinn's pen and pretended to draw on the board with it like a teacher. Hold on I thought, what's this on the pen? A button? I had never noticed this before. It was a blue button, the same shade as the pen and blended in perfectly. I wondered what it would do, I thought. What would happen if I pressed it? I guessed it might do something fancy to the board, but it was just a small button, so it couldn't do anything bad, right? Ok I thought, I am just going to press it. I pressed the button and suddenly a thin metal wire sprung out of the pen and a grapple hook launched out from the end of the wire! And hit the wall! There was a huge bang, mixed with a crack as the wall split.

"What the..." I screamed, as Cian burst into the room and froze to the spot, staring at the pen, or grapple hook, or I guess grapple pen.

"What the..." said Cian, as Jaiden burst into the room and froze right next to Cian.

"What is that?" they both shouted.

"I… I think it's a grapple hook, grapple pen I mean" I replied.

Jaiden said, "I think you were right George, something strange is definitely going on".

Surprisingly Miss Quinn didn't appear to notice the big grapple pen shaped crack in the wall when she came to get us. As expected, we were shifted into the library to do a quiz, as something was going on in our classroom, but Miss Quinn was a bit cagey about what. We were telling Harry about the grapple pen and obviously he didn't believe us, when we noticed that we had been left without any teacher supervision.

"Where did Miss Quinn go" I said.

"Shhhhhh" said Mia "You will get us in trouble".

"There is no one here to get in trouble with, Miss Quinn has disappeared!" I hissed back.

Mia replied, "No she……." looking around "oh my god, she has gone, where did she go".

"More to the point, where did any of the adults go?!" chipped in Harry.

Bethan said crossly "Be Quiet guys, you will get us in trouble!"

We all stared at her and shouted back "There is no one here!".

You have to understand that this is really strange, teachers don't usually leave their classes alone without any adult supervision, they get in trouble for that. We were not quite sure what to do and figured that Miss Quinn would probably be back soon and that we better get on with the quiz, or we really would be in trouble.

Just as I finished my last quiz question five words mysteriously appear on the interactive whiteboard screen; HAVE YOU FINISHED YOUR QUIZ? We all stared blankly at each other; the board had never done that before.

"Perhaps it's some new whizzy teacher technology" Harry suggests. He has an answer for everything.

So, we all got up and headed for the library door to find a teacher. Now, the library door operates by a button from the inside that you press to let yourself out. If you are outside the library then you can only get in if you are a school member of staff and flash your ID card at the little square thing by the door. Anyway, I pressed the open button, but the door didn't open. I tried it again, and again, and again. Starting to get annoyed, I pressed the button slowly, then fast, lightly and then quickly and then I held it down hard for a long time. It still didn't open. Kids had started gathering behind me by this time.

"What's taking so long?" said someone from my class, I forget who.

"The button is broken!" I shouted back.

Other kids came and had a go at the button, thinking that they somehow had the magic touch. I rolled my eyes. When we realised that we were locked in the library, there was complete silence for around 10 seconds and then everyone descended into panic and started shouting all sorts of things like; "Are we locked in?! Where did Miss Quinn go! My computers not working! What's wrong with the button! Will we starve to death! Are there vents in here? We could suffocate!" You get the idea!

Leaving the other kids to panic over the exit button, I walked over to where Harry and Cian were sitting. They were both talking at the same time, but they didn't look worried.

"Hey George" Harry said "Who do you think locked us in?"

I stopped and thought for a while, remembering how angry the teachers appeared to be, especially Miss Quinn.

"Miss Quinn" I replied confidently.

Cian and Harry looked at each other and then at me, and then burst out laughing.

"Ha, you… you actually think someone locked us in George" Harry said whilst laughing and pointing at me.

"Someone didn't lock us in George. They wouldn't lock us in, that's crazy" Cian said "the button is just stuck" they giggled.

I started to think that perhaps they were right. My dad does tell me that I have an overactive imagination. Just then part of the wall suddenly moved, turning in a full circle and pushing myself, Harry and Cian into a dark room. I am not going to lie; it was pretty scary. Thankfully the lights turned on, and I realised that we were not in a room, but at the top of a staircase, that looked very long. We jumped forwards as the door turned a circle again and a big dark and wide shape came looming over to us. We realised what it was…

Chapter Three
No, it's definitely not my imagination!

The rest of the class! Some of them were screaming and some yelling "what's happened? Where are we? Whose there?".

"Who is there?" came again but this time from a recognisable voice; Miss Quinn.

Miss Quinn came into view and she looked worried and startled to see us.

"How did you get here? You should be in the library" She tried to calmly ask.

We explained about the library and wall just moving, taking us to this strange place.

"Oh dear, the electronics are playing up again" Miss Quinn said to herself.

"You need to go immediately" ordered Miss Quinn "you don't need to be here".

"No!" says Flynn, a usually laid-back kid in my class.

"We wanna know where we are! And how we even got here?" Flynn demanded.

"That's none of your business" Miss Quinn snapped "Now go" she demanded as she reached over to pull a lever that I guessed would take us back to the library.

"No!" another kid shouted from the back, and then another yelled "we won't go!"

This started a sort of revolution and soon enough we are all chanting "we won't go, we won't go". Miss Quinn finally succumbed to the pressure of 32 9- and 10-year olds shouting at her.

She sighed and said "alright, alright, calm down kids, you can look around for a little while but just don't touch."

"YAY!" the class cheered interrupting her.

"What the...?" Mrs Hollings said as she poked her head around a door.

"Hi Mrs Hollings" we all shouted as we piled into that room, almost knocking her over.

We all suddenly froze and looked around. The place was amazing! There were computers and high-tech looking guns and other cool looking stuff everywhere. There were teachers with VR headsets on and weird glass rooms which I think were simulation rooms.

There were also buttons, lots of buttons, buttons everywhere! Now, let me tell you the thing about me and buttons; I really really really REALLY like pressing buttons. I once turned off the lights in the school hall and Mrs Chapel made me move my name down. In mum's car, it is torture, she has got this new Hyundai, which is great but it has like a million buttons! I just have to press the window button that makes the window go up and down, just so that I can press a button for once. I guess I don't really have to explain as we have already had the grapple pen incident. Anyway, there were a lot of buttons in the room and my hand started to twitch. Not a good sign. Don't do it George I told myself but my mind and body appeared to have some kind of argument and were not talking to each other anymore. I walked over to a big red button (of course it was big and red – had to be). A big red button. Aren't red buttons usually bad? Especially the big ones? Oh no oh no oh no I thought as my hand started to reach for the button. It was around 5 seconds until there was hand button contact, they went like this:

5 – Need to stop.

4 – somebody help

3 – stop

2 – stupid hand

1 – dam it!

And then BEEEEEEEEEEPPPPPP!

Everybody turned to look at me.

BEEEEEEEEEEEEEEEEEEEEEEEEEEP!

This is bad I thought.

BBEEEEEEEEEEEEEEEEEEEEEEEEEEEEEEP!

It got louder.

BEEEEEEEEEEEEEEEEEEEEEEEEEEEEEEEEEEEEEEEEEEP!

Well, I thought, things couldn't get much worse and then the floor around me gave way, apart from the tile I was standing on. Yes, that's right, it just fell away. I really hate myself sometimes.

"You are very lucky George" Said Mr Walsh appearing behind me out of nowhere.

As he helped get me off of the tile and onto safe ground, he explained, "If we had perfected that button, you would have either fallen to your death or been blown up".

Mr Walsh is one of my favourite teachers, probably the best. When I had him in Year 3, he was so nice and tolerant, and you don't find that in most teachers.

"What?" I answered confused and still a little shaken.

"If you press that button it blows up the nearest intruder in the room" Mr Walsh explained.

"Oh, so I am an intruder?" I asked.

"Yes, because you snuck in here without permission" Mr Walsh replied.

"But Miss Quinn gave me and the rest of the class permission to come in here" I explained matter of factly.

All eyes turned on Miss Quinn, not for the first time that day. Miss Quinn Winced.

"And….." I said, leaving a pause for dramatic effect "I found a grapple pen in her classroom. I want answers!"

"Jo!" said Mrs Stevens another teacher appearing from nowhere (I'm not sure how they kept doing that!).

"Jo, you were meant to deactivate that!" she said.

"and we were locked in the library! why?" shouted Mia.

"Alright" said Mr Hoare "we will tell you, but firstly I am sorry that you were locked in the library, we had an emergency situation to deal with and it was for your protection."

We all stared at the teachers in amazement, waiting for Mr Hoare to tell us more.

Mr Hoare continued "we will tell you, but you must NEVER" he raised his voice when he said this "you must NEVER tell anyone, not another soul, do you understand?"

We all said "Yes!" in chorus.

"Well" he continued "we work for a secret intelligence…"

"Like SHEILD!" laughed someone at the back.

"No, not like SHIELD" Mr Hoare laughed dryly.

"The secret intelligence of teachers agency that now everyone knows about" Joked another kid (name not important to the plot).

"No!!" replied Mr Hoare, losing his patience.

"No, we work for an intelligence agency that was created when they came" he hesitated and then said "they are the Key Finders, and they are searching for keys".

Every teacher in the room physically flinched at hearing the words; Key Finders.

"To unlock what?" asked Harry "A treasure chest or something?"

"No" Mr Hoare replied "to unlock greatness, power and glory."

"You mean a real physical key though, right?" asked Cian.

"Yes, a real key, to unlock a powerful machine, a kind of weapon, luckily he has neither the machine or the key but we fear he is getting close" Mr Hoare continued with a sigh "Look, I really should not be telling you all about this, it's not safe. We don't know exactly what the machine does for sure, its purpose or why it was created, what we do know is that it's just not safe".

"Who is he, and who, who created this machine?" I asked the question that everyone was thinking.

Mr Walsh stepped in appearing to see how hard this was for Mr Hoare and continued; "This, children, is the biggest mystery of all, we have no idea as to how it was created or who created it. The 'he' Mr Hoare spoke of, is" (dramatic pause again but this time I don't think it was for dramatic effect). Gravely, Mr Walsh said "His name is Deadlock and he is the leader of the key finders, and he is the bad guy who wants to fix something that happened in the past, but you cannot change the past, that's basic physics. He stole some valuable information from us and it's put us all in a rather bad mood" he muttered something else and it trailed of, and then he said "and that's all you need to know".

In my mind I was thinking 'WOOOOAAAHHHH' I know that this is a shock so let me recap and let it sink in. The teachers have basically just told us that they are part of a secret intelligence agency of teachers that are trying to stop this guy Deadlock. Deadlock who Mr Walsh says is a bad guy; basically, meaning he is the criminal mastermind, the ultimate villain, the evil one who goes by many names but mainly known as Deadlock. Okay, I am getting carried away but you get the idea. He leads the Key Finders and is looking for a key to unlock some all-powerful machine that is seemingly bad news.

"Well" said a voice, and everyone turned around to see Miss Nunn, the Head Teacher stood in the doorway "that is all very interesting, but are these children meant to be here?" she stated in an annoyed tone.

"Jo, let them in" Mr Hoare said.

Mrs Nunn turned to Miss Quinn, who was scowling at Mr Hoare. I think I saw a smug smile pass his face but I can't be sure.

"Did you Jo?" asked Mrs Nunn.

"Yes" signed Miss Quinn, looking a bit deflated.

"You" Miss Nunn turned to stare at Mr Hoare and Mr Walsh "you were telling the children classified information, and therefore have broken the rules as well (one point to Miss Quinn). I am sure you both understand that these kids could do a lot of damage to our operation. I mean just look at what George Port has just done to the floor. We will have to do another sponsored race of some kind to pay for that!"

In her anger, she clearly forgot we were there with that last comment. I tried to explain that it was the buttons fault but she ignored me, clearly angrier with the teachers.

Miss Nunn continued "What if they tell their parents? We cannot have children anywhere near this operation, it would be chaos!".

Miss Nunn looked really stressed and said "just get them out of here!".

"Come on class, let's go shall we" said Miss Quinn and ushered us out of the room. She made this unfortunate event seem so cheerful that I couldn't help but smile.

"What just happened? I asked Harry as we walked.

"Well, let's see, we accidently stumbled across a secret intelligence that nobody knows about, under our school and our teachers are spies! And there is an evil guy called Deadlock that they are rivalling…it's all pretty hard to ignore and believe" Harry replied.

"Hey Harry" I whispered "do you want to hang back and explore?"

He considered this for a moment "fine" he eventually said.

"No one's forcing you" I said, "Ask Cian the same thing, and ask Cian to ask Jaiden"

Harry turned to Cian, who turned to Jaiden. Harry then turned back to me and said "they are both in".

"Now class" Miss Quinn said "let's go".

Miss Quinn pressed a button and we all dived forward just in time to avoid the wall.

"Quick" I shouted to the others "before anyone notices we are gone".

We leaped down the steps and there were multiple doors.

"Let's not take the first one" said Cian "but what about this one?" he pointed at an iron door.

"I can't hear any voices inside" explained Harry, as he pressed his ear up against the door. And so, we walked in…………………

Chapter Four
I just can't help pushing buttons!

Woah! I thought everything else was high tech but this room, was awesome. There were some stairs which in our eagerness we jumped down them 2 steps at a time. There were loads of screens and even more buttons! Now you would have thought I would have learnt my lesson with the whole exploding floor episode but no. Before I knew it, I had ran over to a set of multi coloured buttons and slammed my hands down on them.

BEEP! BOOP! BLEEP! BLOOP! Sounds came from the equipment, and then "SYSTEM OVERRIDE" said a robotic voice. Oh dear, I thought. "MALFUNCTION, MALFUNCTION" the voice continued. I was starting to freak out.

"Well done, George" said Cian "you have broken the room!"

Red lights flashed all around us and the voice grew louder and said, "SECURITY LEVEL 0 TO 5!" I had no idea what this meant, but I guessed it was nothing good.

All of a sudden, there was an enormous bang and what looked like automatic guns burst out of the walls. We all stared at each other in shock and all appeared to be frozen to the spot until Cian shouted "Quick run!". We all quickly ran straight for the door. My heart pounded. I had never run so fast in my life. Mrs Hollings once told us about this thing called fight or flight. It's where this caveman part of our brain reacts to something and all the blood goes to your arms and legs. This is because if something is chasing you, you either stay and confront it (fight) or run away (flight). I was pretty sure that this was a 'flight' kind of situation.

We didn't even take time to actually open the door. We just ran into it and it opened.

"Hey, what's that noise?" we heard Mrs Sullivan say behind us, sticking her head around a door way.

"That's the security alarm, stupid!" answered Miss D. Miles, appearing from nowhere.

Then loads of teachers started piling out of the door. Our caveman instincts kicked in again and we started sprinting.

"Get them!" shouted one of the teachers.

Suddenly it felt like all the teachers in the school were chasing us. In fact, I didn't even know there were so many teachers. I was feeling pretty frightened by this time. They all looked very cross and a cross teacher is nothing to laugh at, believe me I know!

"Quick!" I shouted.

Oh no, I thought as I spotted more teachers behind a corner. Where *were* they all coming from?

"We're trapped!" screamed Jaiden.

"You are" shouts Miss Scott triumphantly "now move your name down the learning ladder!"

"What?" replied Harry.

Miss Scott looked embarrassed, as she clearly forgot that she wasn't in the classroom or in fact teaching at that point. Despite, myself and what I said earlier about not laughing at cross teachers, I found myself laughing out loud. Cian, Harry and Jaiden joined in my laughing and we all looked at each other whilst laughing with unsure looks on our faces.

"Oh, stop this childish insolence" shouted Miss Nunn, as she stepped out of the crowds of teachers.

Now obviously if I was being really insolent, I would have replied that we are children so by definition would be childish, but I thought better of it.

Miss Nunn continued "You should not be here, now go!"

Some teachers came up to escort us to the exit and one pressed the same lever as Miss Quinn did and the door opened. We arrived just as Miss Quinn was finishing delivering a stern warning to the class. The warning included the usual secret spy stuff, if you know what that is. Stuff like: you must never tell anyone about today, you must never use that door again, etc etc. Basically, they think we are just dumb kids who will forget this. One of the teachers explained to Miss Quinn that we were found in the 'camera room" and that we were 'sneaking around, causing trouble'. The teachers exchange worried looks. Miss Quinn took us back to class whilst muttering something about too much stress for one day.

When mum picks me and my brother Henry up from school, she always asks how our day was. And that is what she is asking me right now – "how was your day George?"

"Oh, it was…completely normal thanks mum, absolutely nothing happened, you know just a normal day at school, maths, literacy, reading and spellings" I reply, telling myself in my head to 'play it cool George, don't overdo it!'.

"Yep yep, all fine" I continue "good, had fun, you know normal".

"I see" replies mum with a smile.

Chapter Five
Training Montage

So, for a while things returned back to normal and no one spoke about the teacher/spy incident. Mum has just dropped me and my little brother Henry off at school and I can already sense that something is not right. I press the breakfast club bell and we wait to be let in. And we wait. And we wait. And we wait. No one comes to let us in and mum has already left. These teachers are really testing my patience now.

Henry looks to me and says "George, where are the teachers?".

Alright, I've had enough. I am going to force the double doors open. Geez, this is HARD! C`mon…just a little more…yes! I've done it and we are in! I can hear shouting coming from, well, everywhere. I take Henry up to the year 5 and 6 section and I see a few kids that Henry knows there and ask them to look after him whilst I find out what is going on. I need to find Harry, Cian and Jaiden. Actually, I could ask the teachers…. but where are they come to think of it? I search around the school looking for signs of any teachers, but they are nowhere to be found. More children start arriving at school, their parents dropping them off at the gate and unaware that there are no staff inside! Children walk around looking confused and end up just sitting in groups talking and appearing unsure of what to do.

I eventually find Harry, Cian and Jaiden in our classroom, with a group of other kids, looking up at the whiteboard. Scrawled on the whiteboard is a single word; Deadlock!

Next to the word is a picture of a key. I remember that day when Mr Walsh told us about Deadlock and the Key Finders. My blood ran cold. Loads of questions raced through my head: What is going on? Has Deadlock taken the teachers? If so, why has he left such a dumb clue behind? Are we in danger? What should we do?

Miss Quinn's class (my class) took control and lead all the children into the main hall. Harry pushed me forward to address all of the children.

"Make it good George!" encouraged Jaiden in a rather unhelpful way.

I would like to say that I made a great speech about how we were going to rescue the teachers and defeat Deadlock and all the children cheered my name. However, what really happened was that I turned around and pushed Harry in front who just said "start training montage!".

We entered the secret base though the library and started training (Cian helpfully found the training room). The training involved laser guns, code breaking, the art of disguise and ninja moves (taught by my little bro Henry: all he did was run around and say "ninja ninja" but it seemed to work). This went on for a few days. Do you know how we did this? We found a device in the secret base labelled 'Protocol Supply Teacher'. When activated, it displays holograms of teachers all over school. The parents were fooled when dropping us off and picking us up each day. The training was going great. We were ready for action, and feeling quite tired.

Chapter 6
We're clueless!

Right now, I am practising my laser skills and getting pretty good, if I do say so myself. I am having so much fun that I almost forget the situation I am in.

Suddenly, Mia comes up to me and asks "why are we doing all this training? When we could be out looking for Deadlock?".

"What?" I reply as I shoot my gun and it narrowly misses Cian's head!

"Hey!" shouts Cian "I just gelled my hair this morning!".

"Oops, sorry Cian!" I say, "I mistook you for a training dummy!".

"Who are you calling a dummy, dummy!" Cian shouts but is half laughing.

I then realise that Mia is right, we *are* clueless. I mean we have no clues. There is not a clue in sight. I feel pretty stupid for doing all this training and we don't actually know where the Key Finders are!

"Right" I say, calling everyone over "we need to look for clues".

So, we all started searching the school but mainly the secret lab. As it turns out, Miss Nunn (The Head Teacher) has a secret door in her office leading to another office. How many offices does one person need? There are bound to be clues in here I thought. Looking... looking... looking... aha! A filing cabinet labelled; Nothing interesting here.

Humm, 'Nothing Interesting here'. This looks suspicious to me and like something I would write to stop people looking in the cabinet. Miss Nunn is a clever person. I am going to take a look inside. I hope it doesn't explode, like the floor did before. I cautiously open it and find to my surprise a load of files about Briary Primary School just down the road. This is odd as clearly; we are Hampton Primary School not Briary so why would Mrs Nunn be so interested in all this information. The more I read, the more I know. I notice a file marked 'plans' and inside are some blue prints of underneath Briary School. Is it another teacher base I wonder? Or just could it be the base of the Key Finders? Quickly I find the others and inform them of my findings.

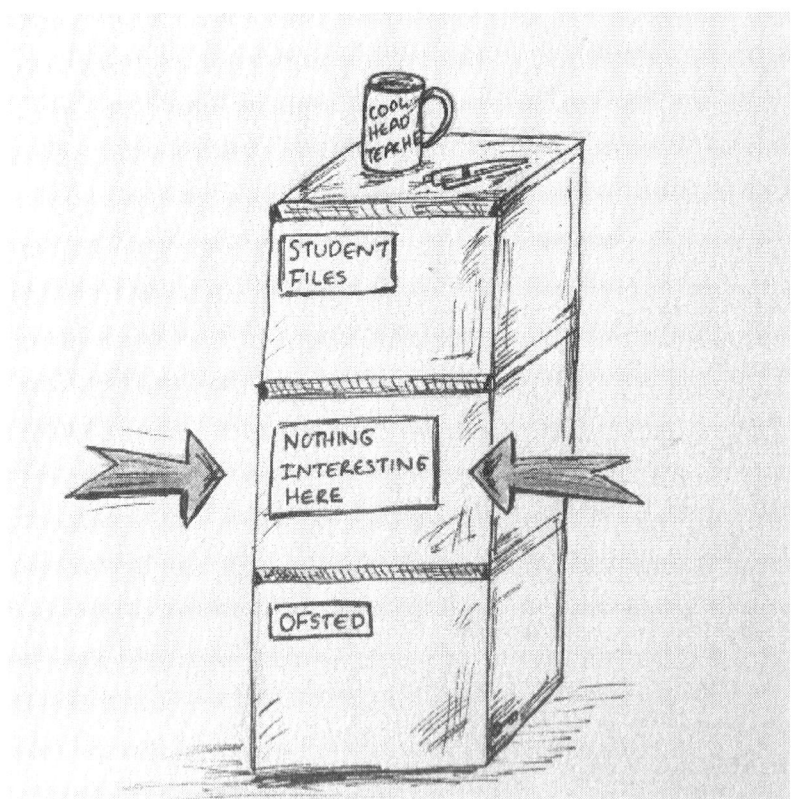

Jaiden says "I always knew that Briary school was a bit sinister".

"No, you didn't" said Harry "or you would have said already Jaiden!".

Cian interrupted by saying "Well, what are we waiting for, we need to go there then!".

I reminded them that we are meant to be at school and four kids walking around out there on a school day would be spotted and someone would phone the Police.

"I have an idea!" shouted Harry excitedly.

Chapter 7
The wheels on the bus go around and round

So, we are in disguise, we have found two giant coats and Cian is sitting on my shoulders, and Harry is sitting on Jaiden's shoulders. Did I mention that we are sitting in the school mini bus and Harry is at the wheel, trying to drive. *Trying* being the correct word! It seemed like a good idea at the time to get to Briary undetected, but now I am not so sure.

"No offence Harry but you are a terrible driver!" I yell while holding on for dear life.

Up ahead I can see a zebra crossing and an old lady is crossing it painfully slowly.

"Harry stop!" I shout.

"What?" replies Harry "I can't hear you?".

"I said STOP!!" I yell.

"Alright alright, no need to shout".

Harry says as he pulls to a stop just in time. My heart is racing. To our surprise, the old lady opens the mini bus door and gets in. She appears to think it's her bus. We have no time to explain and so she comes along for the ride.

We hear a little yelp from the back of the minibus.

"What was that?" says Cian.

We all look back to see that the old lady had sat on Henry. Wait a minute, Henry!

"What is Henry doing on the bus?" we all say at exactly the same time.

"Oh, I am sorry young man" says the old lady "I appear to be sitting on you."

Henry squeezes out from behind the old lady and explains that he wanted to come along and help.

"He can't help!" shouts Harry "what is he, like 5 years old?".

"Nearly 6 actually" says Henry whilst sticking his tongue out at Harry.

"You have not seen my brother in full rage mode" I say "He goes crazy. He could be useful, and we can't take him back now; we are nearly at Briary".

We pull up into Briary Primary School car park in one piece, amazingly (Harry's driving really is terrible).

Chapter 8
This is crazy, you won't believe it!

Before we get out of the mini bus, I say "guys, if we are going to do this, we need a team name".

Cian replies "George we have been through this, we don't do team names!".

The others nod along in agreement with Cian.

"Well, if we are basically saving the world, I think having a team name is appropriate!" I reply.

"Well, I don't" says Cian.

"Well I do".

"Well I still don't".

"Well I still do".

"We could be called 'Small Spies'" says Jaiden.

"No way" says Harry.

"Let's just settle with that for now – Small Spies it is" I say.

"Ok' everyone sighs.

"We also need a code word if anything goes wrong and we need to pull out the training moves" I suggest.

"Like what?" says Jaiden.

Henry pops up and says "Training montage!"

"Yes, training montage is the code word, or words".

"Great" we all say together.

First thing we notice is kids staring at us through the windows.

"That's not good" says Harry.

Everything *seems* normal, but I think we have all learnt by now that when things appear normal, there is usually something up. So, we walk towards the building cautiously.

"Hey guys, maybe we should pretend we are school inspectors?" I suggest "we still have our long coats".

"Good idea" says Harry "but what will we do with Henry?"

Before anyone can reply Henry jumps inside one of the coats and completely disappears. That will do.

Suddenly one of the teachers walks up to us, seemingly out of nowhere (how do teachers keep doing that?).

"I am Miss Keyley, and who are you?" says the teacher.

"We" says Harry in an important sounding voice "we are school inspectors straight from Ofsted. Did you not know we were coming?"

Miss Keyley looks slightly shocked but gathers herself together and says "well, erm, please do come along".

As soon as we are in the building and Miss Keyley isn't looking, we make a run for it. We find the library and hide behind a large bookcase to decide our next move. Strangely but helpfully, the library is empty.

"Have you noticed that there are signs everywhere saying no scissors? Millions of them! Why would a school not allow any scissors, how do they do crafts and stuff?" Says Jaiden.

Before we are able to think about this, suddenly, we hear someone open the library door and run in, so Jaiden takes a peek.

"It's that Miss Keyley." he says.

Miss Keyley almost bumps into another teacher.

She says "Mr Interlock, there are intruders in the school! We need to get to the CCTV room!"

We watch as they Miss Keyley pulls a book out from one of the shelves and a passage opens up in the wall.

"I think we've all learnt a valuable lesson from this." whispered Harry.

"What's that?" I say.

"That all secret bases are accessed through libraries, obviously." I snorted, just a little bit too loudly, and Miss Keyley and Mr Interlock turned around and looked in our direction and started heading our way. I had to think quick. Just then I remembered Henry was under the coat.

I poked my head in and said "Henry, remember the ninja moves? Can you do some for me?"

Immediately, Henry runs out in front of the teachers, jumping around and shouting "Ninja! Ninja!".

Miss Keyley and Mr Interlock look confused and Miss Keyley says "What on earth is this insolent child doing here?".

"Insolent! INSOLENT!" shouts Henry and leaps at them in full rage mode.

"I told you he would be useful." I say.

This gives us the opportunity to run away down the not-so-secret passage.

Chapter 9
The Cliff-hanger Chapter

Well, the secret passage way leads to a base that looks pretty similar to the one at Hampton. We sneak around, avoiding teachers, who appear to be looking for intruders (us). We come to 3 doors. I put my ear up to the first one and I can hear footsteps and voices inside. Not that one! I approach door 2 and listen in. Same as door 1. Before I can approach door 3, Jaiden has already opened it and run straight in. Such a Jaiden thing to do, I think to myself.

Luckily, the room is empty, well sort of. There are computers (or possibly even super-computers).

"Well, there are a lot of buttons, George" says Cian "I think this is your area" he laughs.

He is right and I just can't help myself and I start pushing buttons. Nothing really happens at first but then a large screen projects onto the wall. It was some kind of plan. By looking at the plan I now know that the powerful machine and key to unlock it are both hidden at…. dun dun duuunnn! Hampton Primary school!!! My school!

"Hold on" says Harry after this discovery "are Miss Keyley and Mr Interlock and maybe all the teachers at Briary the evil Key Finders?"

"Well, duh, Harry!" says Jaiden "just look at their names! Also, I saw a sign on the Head teacher's door that said Mr Deadlock".

"Why didn't you say?!" I shout.

"Well, George, we were a bit busy running at that point." He replied.

So, for you readers, just to recap. We have discovered that the teachers at Briary school are actually the Key Finders and have a secret plan to find the machine and key to unlock, that is hidden somewhere in Hampton Primary school. Miss Nunn (Hampton's Head Teacher) must have been onto them as she had all that information about Briary in her secret office. However, Mr Walsh told us that they did not know much about the machine which suggests that the teachers at Hampton do not know that it is there. So, my guess is that Mr Deadlock (obviously the evil mastermind, one in the same – keep up readers!) has our teachers held prisoners so that they can go and find the machine at Hampton without anyone stopping them. What they did not bank on was SMALL SPIES stopping them. It was up to us now.

At that very second, we hear the door creak open and a tall figure is suddenly standing in the doorway, blocking any escape.

"Hello children" says the stranger in a sinister sounding voice "I am Mr Deadlock."

Chapter 10

The Fight Scene, in which a lot of fighting happens

We stand there in shock, frozen to the spot like statues. Deadlock takes a step further into the room. We all take a step back. It all goes tense. Deadlock takes another step towards us and we take another step back. It's a bit like dancing but ten times more dangerous.

"Wh-where are all our teachers?" says Harry.

Deadlock considers this for a moment and then replies "And why would I tell you that?"

Deadlock pulls out a laser gun from his back pocket and points it at us and demands "Now why are you here?"

"Why are you asking?" I say in my most annoying voice.

Deadlock snarls at us but also looks a little amused. He really is evil. "You are playing a dangerous game little ones." He says to us.

"You are playing a dangerous game little ones." I repeat back to him in a mocking voice.

Deadlock growls "Don't push it."

"I think I just have." I say, not quite sure what I am doing.

Whatever my tactic, it seems to be working just a little bit too well. He gets so angry that he pins me up against the back wall.

"You'll regret that." He says, putting the laser gun up against the side of my head

"Any last words?"

"Yes actually" I reply "Training montage."

At this, the others leap into action and all attack Deadlock at once. His hand slips and he shoots a hole into the ceiling. I am glad it was the ceiling and not me.

"Go for the shins! I hear they break easily!" Jaiden shouts whilst holding onto Deadlock's leg.

"Where did you learn that?" shouts Harry whilst punching Deadlock in the back of the head.

"During training, obviously!" shouts Jaiden back.

I manage to knock the laser gun out of Deadlock's hand and he whacks me in the head in return.

Obviously realising that we were not going to let up our attack, Deadlock forces us off and then runs towards a wall. Just before he gets there, he knocks a button and a secret door (they are all over the place) opens up and he leaps though it. We hear him shout something evil about getting revenge one day and then he is gone. The wall suddenly closes up before any of us can get through.

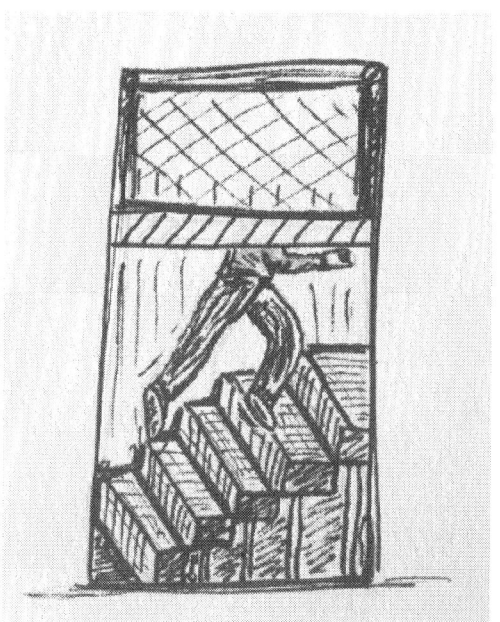

Chapter 11
The end, but leaving it open for a sequel

"What do we do now?" shouts Cian.

"Well, he's gone" I reply, still trying to catch my breath "there is not much we can do, we need to find our teachers and warn them".

We head back the way we entered and start looking around for any sign of the teachers. Its strangely quiet with no sign of Briary teachers, or should I say Key Finders. This is worrying as it must mean that they are on their way to Hampton, which is filled with innocent children, including Jaiden and Cian's younger brothers! Talking of younger brothers, just then Henry appears out of nowhere.

"Thank god you are ok" I say, realising that I was actually a bit worried about him "how did you get away from Miss Keyley and Mr Interlock?"

"Never mind that George, I found the teachers!" says Henry, looking happy with himself.

"Well done Henry! You little ninja legend!" I say.

We follow Henry around loads of what seem like endless tunnels. We eventually find what can only be described as a dungeon! And behind some huge metal bars are all the teachers, looking a bit bruised (their bodies and their egos, I think).

"George, Cian, Jaiden, Harry and Henry! How did you find us?" says Miss Nunn.

She has a huge smile on her face so I don't think she is cross.

"Erm, well you know, we just battled Mr Deadlock to try and find you" Harry says.

Before Miss Nunn can ask any more questions, I say "We think Deadlock is headed to Hampton as we speak. How do we get you out of here?".

"There's a key in that safe over there, but I didn't see what the code was" says Mr Walsh.

Miss Quinn jumps up and says "I do, I do, I watched that awful Miss Keyley punch in the code and memorised it".

"Did you, Miss Quinn? Remind me to give you a pay rise after all this." says Miss Nunn.

I was glad about this as we did get Miss Quinn in trouble before when we sneaked into the Hampton base. Seems like she's back in the good books now. We punch in the code, that releases the key and let out the teachers. We all run and pile into the minibus. There's obviously too many of us for one little mini bus but we somehow manage to squeeze in, even with the old lady still sitting there (must get her back home safely later). Miss Nunn was at the wheel this time thankfully, much to Harry's protest. We drive so fast that I need to hold on so tight that my knuckles turn white.

We reach the school and the gates are closed! We can also see that all the other Hampton school children are in the playground, trapped under a giant cage of some kind. For dramatic effect, Miss Nunn puts her foot down on the accelerator and drives straight at the gates, crashing through them with great speed.

"THAT WAS AWESOME!" we all shout in unison.

"Get behind us children! We have a school to save!" shouts Miss Nunn.

She has a determined look in her face of a true hero, and despite the many times I have visited her office, I have never seen that look. I hope Ofsted are watching (apart from the dangerous speeding through the gates bit).

We obey Miss Nunn and walk a little behind her and the other teachers. We enter the school and head straight to the hall. I notice that the teachers are looking around a lot, as if we are going to be ambushed at any second now. Come to think of it, we probably are going to be ambushed at any second now. Wait a minute...WE ARE PROBABLY GOING TO BE AMBUSHED AT ANY SECOND NOW!! Just then we are surprised by an ambush of Briary teachers (didn't see that coming).

We're now face to face with Deadlock (dunno how he got here), a load of mean looking Briary teachers and a whole lot of laser guns. I'll be honest with you; I am not sure where the plot is going to go here. It seems although we are doomed.

"I demand you leave my school immediately!" commands Miss Nunn fiercely.

"My dear Yvonne," Deadlock says in a sickly-sweet tone "I think you will find that this school belongs to me now".

Feeling brave, I step forward and say "He only wants the school because the machine and key to unlock it are hidden here at Hampton".

Everyone gasps in surprise, apart from Deadlock who is aware of this fact.

Now, readers, can we just pause there so that I can describe Deadlock to you. I've just realised that you do not know what any of the characters look like, but I think it is important that you get the whole picture of what true evil villain looks like. It was a bit dark when we saw him in the last chapter so it seems right to do it now. So, he has beady little eyes that are a light shade of grey, one of which has a scar that runs through his eyebrow straight down to the bottom of his nose, so it actually goes straight through his eye. Hey, wait a minute...I have just realised something; when I was running with scissors the other week, one of the teachers said "Stop running with those, you don't want to get Deadlocked!". I was unsure what they meant at the time and thought it best not to ask an angry teacher. I guess I now know how Deadlock got the injury. A headteacher running with scissors! That is *not* a good look.

Deadlock has a long, crooked nose which sticks out at a strange angle for at least 2 inches. He has a strange sly smile that shows, even when he is not happy, just like now. He is also really muscly and I would not want to get into a fight with him. Wait hold on a minute, I think I've already done that.

Right, back to the story. Everyone is still gasping about the revelation that the machine and key are at Hampton somewhere. Suddenly I get an excellent idea. Whilst Miss Nunn and Deadlock start to argue about whose school it is, I sneak out of the hall. I run to the playground to find the children still locked in the cage, looking confused. To my surprise. It's not locked but there is a big latch on the top of the cage, that they can't reach. I climb to the top. It's not too much trouble for me as I love climbing and I am actually pretty good at it. I undo the latch but then have to pull the children out one by one, which is tiring but children start to help me once they are out. We free the children and I explain the situation and ask them to sneak into their own classrooms to find some secret weapons (I tell them what they are but I am not telling you for suspense purposes) and meet me back in the hall.

I run to Miss Quinn's classroom myself to find my secret weapons and luckily, I find a whole pot of them. I run back to the hall and stealthily hand them out to my friends quickly (even though still engaged in an argument, Deadlock is looking curious). Once I see that most of the children are back with their weapons I shout "ATTACK!".

All the children spring forward with scissors (sharp end pointing out!) pointing at Deadlock. Deadlock looks more frightened than a mouse caught in cat's claws. He screams a long blood curdling scream and we all laugh at him.

Deadlock shouts "It's not funny! This is traumatic! I hate SCISSORS! What kind of school is this!?"

Then Deadlock runs out of the school screaming and holding his eye. The Briary teachers (or Key Finders) look unsure what to do and realising that they have no leader, run away after him. All the Hampton teachers and children cheer!

Miss Nunn turns to me, Jaiden, Harry, Cian and Henry. She looks angry and says "You boys put yourselves in awful danger!"

Then she smiles and says "but you saved us all and I am very proud of you". All the teachers and children clapped and cheered us. It was amazing.

Miss Nunn addresses the entire hall "Now, everyone, if it is true that the powerful machine and key to unlock it is somewhere here at our school, then we must not look for it. That's right, we must leave it be, as its power is unknown and better left alone. Our job as a school, united in Hampton values, is to protect the machine at any cost. We must all be on guard and protect our school!"

Everyone cheers.

Miss Nunn continues "Now on a more serious note, you are all part of this now children, which means that you must keep our secret and never ever tell your parents or anyone else about this. Is this clear?!" Everyone nods. "You are now formally the Undercover Kids of Hampton!" Everyone cheers again.

"Undercover Kids!" Harry says "that's a great team name, why didn't you think of that George!?"

"Alright, alright" I reply.

Myself, Jaiden, Harry and Cian stand in a circle put our hands on top of each other and shout "Undercover Kids forever!". It was a little lame to be honest.

"Right" interrupts Miss Quinn "it's nearly home time, parents will be here soon and there is an old lady in the reception asking to be taken home".

"Yes, yes," says Miss Nunn "back to your classroom's children".

Mum picked us up and asked, as usual "How was your day boys".

I winked at Henry and replied "yep, it was alright, you know just normal school".

And that, was that. From that day on school returned to normal with one change, during lunch breaks the Undercover Kids were allowed down to the secret lab to learn spy techniques, train at ninja school and share intelligence with the teachers. So far Deadlock has not tried to attack again, but if he does, we will be ready.

So, remember kids: Don't run with scissors, you might turn into an evil villain or more likely hurt yourself.

The End…..or is it?!

Printed in Great Britain
by Amazon